Give Us a Great Big Smile, Rosy Cole

Give Us a Great Big Smile, Rosy Cole

Sheila Greenwald

A YEARLING BOOK

Published by
Dell Publishing Co., Inc.
1 Dag Hammarskjold Plaza
New York, New York 10017

Yearling ® TM 913705, Dell Publishing Co., Inc.

ISBN: 0-440-42923-4

Reprinted by arrangement with Little, Brown & Company.
Printed in the United States of America
Third Dell printing—June 1984

CW

To Melanie Kroupa

Chapter One

My name is Rosy Cole and
I'm in a lot of trouble. I've been in trouble

now for six weeks, starting when I turned ten. I have two older sisters named Anitra and Pippa, a mother and a father named Sue and Mike, a cat named Pie, and an uncle Ralph, who is a successful photographer.

Because of Uncle Ralph we are a famous family.

My sister Anitra is thirteen. She studies ballet at the American School of Ballet. Three years ago when she was ten, Uncle Ralph did a book all about her. It was called *Anitra Dances*. It featured photographs of my sister looking cute and adorable and graceful in her tutu and leotard. The words in the book were supposed to sound like Anitra. I'll give you an idea of how this worked out.

In the book, when Anitra finds she didn't get the part of Mary in *The Nutcracker,* she says, "I am always a little sad when I don't get a part I try out for, but then I can learn so much from the person who does get the part because she must be better than I am, and I can improve myself so I'll be ready when my turn comes."

In real life, the day Anitra didn't get the part, she slammed the door and yelled, "That klutz Zora Slonim got the role in *The Nutcracker*. She can't dance her way out of a can of nuts. Pull, it's all pull. She moves like a spastic giraffe."

My sister Pippa is twelve. She is an equestrian. She loves to ride her horse, Doobie, more than anything. Two years ago, when she was ten, Uncle Ralph did a book all about Pippa. It was called *Pippa Prances*. It showed beautiful photographs of Pippa in shows, jumping and galloping and fondling her horse, Doobie.

I have the two books in front of me on my desk. They are big and beautiful and have made my sisters famous and Uncle Ralph "in the dough."

They make me nervous and fre-
quently depressed. *Anitra Dances* and
Pippa Prances. For three years now I
have been thinking, what does Rosy do?
Take Chances? Give Cockeyed Glances?

Okay, so everything was moving along in its normal way until about six weeks ago, when I turned ten. I'm sure you can imagine that ten has been an important birthday in my family. The birth of a new celebrity.

As usual, this landmark event was celebrated at a restaurant called Gino's on the Park. We were all there. Mom, Dad, Anitra, Pippa, Uncle Ralph, and the Nikon. I blew out the candles.

Uncle Ralph aimed his camera and said, "Hey, Rose, Toots, are you or are you not going to be my next best-seller?"

Right then and there I realized I couldn't consider eating my own birthday cake. The piece of icing in my

mouth simply stuck there like Crazy Glue. I excused myself to go to the ladies' room. I was only three feet from the table when I heard Uncle Ralph say to Mom, "Hey, Sis, has she pulled her act together?"

And I heard Mom say, "She's awfully good at drawing pictures, Ralph."

Ralph said, "Doesn't sound very visual. I mean, does she play tennis or swim or — you know what I mean, Sis."

"No, what do you mean, Ralph?"

"I mean I need another book real bad. I mean I am temporarily broke."

"You mean you've gone and lost at the track again," Mom said. "Honestly, Ralph, you are hopeless."

By then I was out of earshot. I spat my icing into the toilet and washed my face and began to cry.

A lady came into the washroom, so I sat down in one of the booths and closed the door and cried privately for the next three minutes. Those were the last good three minutes I can remember. As I

walked up to the table, everybody was looking at me.

Mom said, "Rose, sweetheart, would you mind if Uncle Ralph goes over to watch you when you take your violin lessons this week?"

I didn't answer right away.

Uncle Ralph said, "I just want to see how it looks, Rose, Bush Babes. Just get the feel of it."

Now the truth of the matter is this: I have been taking violin lessons for two years. I go twice a week. I try to miss at least one lesson and arrive late for the other. The first lesson is a quartet. We play chamber music. It's me on violin, Debbie Prusock on viola, Hermione Wong on cello, and Linda Dildine on piano.

Ms. Radzinoff, who runs the School of Music, is an old friend of my mom's from college. Me and Ms. Radzinoff have a secret. We both know that the only reason she keeps teaching me is that my mom is an old friend. I didn't want anybody to learn this secret.

My next lesson was on Tuesday. Monday night I prayed that I would wake up with a terrible cold or a high fever. My prayers were not answered.

"Rosamond, don't forget you're meeting Uncle Ralph at music school," my mother reminded me at breakfast. "I called T.R." — that's Radzinoff — "to make sure it was all right."

Ever since I turned ten, I noticed my family called me Rosamond instead of Rosy.

I go to the Read School. It is a medium-sized private school on one of the side streets on the Upper East Side. I can walk to school. Anitra and Pippa are at a professional children's school. They used to go to Read.

Most mornings I walk to school with Hermione Wong. She is the same Hermione Wong who plays cello at Ms.

Radzinoff's chamber-music class. Lately she has been super-friendly to me.

"Hi, Hermione," I said. "I thought you wouldn't have waited. I'm five minutes late." Hermione is a nut about being prompt.

"That's okay," she said. "I'd rather be late and walk with you. You are my best friend."

"Really?" This was news to me. I always thought I was more her most convenient friend. But I let this pass. We walked for half a block and didn't say anything because there was such a sharp April wind in our faces it was hard to talk.

Then Hermione said, "Say, Rosy, now that you are ten, isn't your uncle Ralph going to do a book about you?"

"I don't know," I said.

"Well, if he does, and I bet he does," Hermione chirped on, "I hope you remember I'm your best friend, and I'd love it if he got a picture of us together, just walking along to school or just talking in the lobby or maybe at my house or maybe just a picture of me carrying my book bag, waiting for you in the lobby."

"He could do a whole book on you," I said, "and call it *A Very Young Bag Lady*."

Hermione pinched her lips together and shot me a very unfriendly look. We did not have any more to say to each other.

In gym class, a girl named Norma Belafont asked me if Uncle Ralph would do any shots of me in school, and to please tell her the day before, because she had this dreamy new dress she would wear.

Every Tuesday and Thursday before I go into the brownstone where Ms. Radzinoff runs her School of Music, I treat myself to a chocolate soda and a Danish. I have this treat at a luncheonette on the corner of Columbus Avenue. It is dark and musty and long. They never modernized it. The linoleum is coming up and the counter top shows dark spots from years of use. The covers

on the stools are cracking. There is an unpleasant lady who stands behind the counter reading the *Daily News*. Behind her is a long mirror that goes the whole length of the counter, so I can sit and watch myself drinking my soda and eating my Danish. I sit there looking at myself and I think, ten beautiful free minutes before I have to go . . . eight wonderful free minutes, seven wonderful free minutes, six fantastic free minutes. Then the soda is gone and the Danish too, and I have to leave, but I've made every minute count.

As I go up the brownstone steps to the School of Music, I feel Dumbness come on me like a heavy coat. I get dumber and dumber on every step, until I am completely DUMB.

Uncle Ralph was already there. He was talking to T.R.

Hermione was unpacking her cello.

Linda and Debbie walked in and made faces as if to say, "What's up?"

T.R. was her usual clipped, unruffled, and, I have to say, nasty self, but I could tell she was kind of excited. She said, "Girls, I want to introduce you to Mr. Ralph LeBow, Rosy's uncle. He will be taking pictures of you while you play today. He would like you to pretend that he is not here at all. He wants you to be as natural and normal as usual."

Right away they looked like this:

We sat down before our music stands and took out our music.

Ms. Radzinoff told us what page to turn to and what measure to begin on. We tuned up.

T.R. counted, one, two, three, and we started to play. Two interesting things happened. First thing, Linda, Hermione, and Debbie were playing horribly.

Second thing, Ms. Radzinoff was trying to cover up for ME. Trying to help me to look good. Usually she glares or stamps and calls me "idiot." But this time she let my mistakes go by, smiling radiantly at me every time I came anywhere near the right note.

She kept stopping to talk to us about the music. "Mozart is so witty here," she said, laughing like a loon. "Listen, you can hear the wit, the fun, the jest." She

sounded like the hostess of a public television children's music special instead of glaring, hissing Teddy Radzinoff.

Uncle Ralph was *click, click, click*ing away as if film cost a penny a roll.

Hermione was sweating like a fighter.

Linda banged the piano as if it had done something horrible to her.

Debbie looked as if she was about to cry.

We kept playing. Worse and worse. I couldn't imagine how anyone who liked music could stand to listen. Ms. Radzinoff must be a secret music hater.

Finally, it was time to pack up and hear Ms. Radzinoff's last words of the day. "Practice the allegro, girls, with special attention to the last five measures. Remember the *humor*. We will take the fourth movement next week."

Uncle Ralph said, "Thanks a lot, kids. You are wonderful, beautiful people, and likewise Ms. Radzinoff."

"Call me Teddy," she said.

"Call me Ralph," he said.

"Call me wonderful," Linda said.

"I'll be back on Thursday, Teddy," said Ralph.

I tried to get out the door fast, but he saw me. "Hey, wait up, Rosy. We have to talk." We went out of the building together.

Usually as I leave the building the dumbness coat is removed from me, and I feel smarter and smarter till I reach the sidewalk where I am myself again. But leaving with Uncle Ralph, I felt rotten all the way to the street.

"Rosy, I like what I saw just now," Ralph said. "The faces, the fiddles, even the sweat on the brows. It all looked good. Of course, I have to develop the prints to see what I get, but I feel in my bones that we've got a winner. I think you're going to be my dark horse."

He stopped in the middle of the sidewalk and put one hand on top of my head and the other under my chin so I had to look into his happy, smiling face. "I never thought I'd get a book out of you, cookie. To be perfectly frank, I thought you'd turn out a dud. But you, Rosy Dotes, are going to come in in first place, a winner. Just when I was about to go B-U-S-T. I'm making bets on you. My next book, *our* next book, will be called . . ." He closed his eyes to think up a title. He looked so happy and excited, the way he looks when a horse he bets on is about to come in first. "It will be called *A Very Little Filly*," he said.

Then he opened his eyes and saw me. "I mean, *Fiddler*."

Chapter Two

And so my fate was sealed. Right away a whole bunch of things in my life changed.

Three girls in my class came up to me separately to tell me they were my best friend.

Teddy Radzinoff called to speak to my mother several times a day.

Uncle Ralph decided to photograph me practicing in my bedroom.

Mom redecorated and carpeted my bedroom.

Uncle Ralph decided to photograph me practicing in the living room.

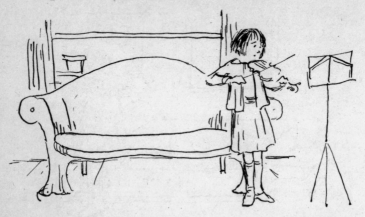

Mom redecorated and carpeted the living room.

I started to keep this private diary.

I started to practice. Uncle Ralph would say, "Okay, sweetheart, I'll just take pictures the way I always do, and you practice the way *you* always do."

What I always did was NEVER PRACTICE.

As a result of my practicing at home, the telephone began to ring. I heard Mom say, "No, we do not have a cat in heat or an electric saw. It must be someone else's apartment."

"Who was that?" I said.

Mom didn't hear me because she had put the plugs back in her ears and turned on the vacuum cleaner.

After the third phone call, Mom took the telephone off the hook. "That Mrs. Rapposo next door is going nuts," Mom said.

I really felt sorry for Mrs. Rapposo. I wished I could stop playing as much as

she wanted me to, but Uncle Ralph said,
"Move over to the window and take that
last part again. The one where
your arm goes back and forth
very fast." He didn't hear
a single thing. He only
saw it. "Give us a
great big smile,
Rosy Cole,"
he said.
"Beautiful."

Mrs. Rapposo was banging on the
front door, hollering. "I'm reporting you
to the landlord, Sue Cole. You can't fool
me. It's a wildcat."

Mom opened the door a crack and
Didi Rapposo stuck her head in. When
she saw me holding my violin, she said,
"Oh, Rosy, dear. I'm so sorry. I didn't
realize it was *you*." She looked upset.

"Maybe we can work out something with soundproofing, Sue," she said to Mom.

They went into the kitchen to talk. The next day Mom had the wall between our apartment and Mrs. Rapposo's apartment carpeted. Every time I met Mrs. Rapposo in the elevator or the hallway, her eyes filled with tears.

One Thursday morning, Hermione was waiting for me in the lobby as usual. But she was in an agitated state. Her skin was splotchy and her eyes looked as if she had a fever. She couldn't seem to keep them on anything for more than a second, even when she was talking to me. They kept shifting around.

"Oh, Rosamond," she said in a shrill voice, "how exciting to be turning into a book. Is your uncle Ralph really going to do you?"

"It looks that way," I said.

"Oh, how can you be so calm about it? If it were me, I'd be in heaven. Remember, please, that I am your very best friend. Also, I photograph like a dream. I've brought some photos of myself to show your uncle Ralph in case he'd like to see how photogenic I am. I wonder if he knows that I sing? Rosy, did you tell him that I sing?"

"No," I said.

Hermione gave me a nasty look which she thought I didn't see. "If you were

really my best friend, you'd mention it to him," Hermione said. We walked for a block before Hermione said, "He never did a book on a singer, did he?"

"No," I said.

"Well, please tell him that I sing at least as well as you play the violin."

"About this best friend stuff," I started to say.

"Oh, Rosy," she interrupted me, "don't tell me we're not. I would just die."

I thought of the old joke, "With friends like you, who needs enemies?"

In school it seemed to me that I was treated differently. I kept thinking that people stopped talking when I passed them. My teacher, Mrs. Winston, gave me lots of odd, long looks, and as we were going up to the library she said, "I never realized that you were musical, Rosamond."

That makes two of us, I thought.

"Perhaps you'd consider playing for us at school sometime," she said sweetly. "Your uncle Ralph has asked if he could take pictures here at the school without causing any disruption. One of our Friday morning assembly programs may be just the right occasion."

"I don't think so," I said. The idea of Uncle Ralph coming to my school was the worst yet. It made me sick to my stomach. But the day wasn't over. I still had to go to the School of Music for my private lesson.

When I went into the soda fountain, Uncle Ralph was sitting on the last stool, drinking black coffee and going over the racing sheet. He saw me right away.

"Hi, Rosy Dotes," he called. The woman behind the counter glared at him. I could see he had already filled an ash-

tray and spilled sugar. Uncle Ralph is always pretty nervous. "I've been waiting for you," he said. "I wanted to go over some stuff with you. What'll you have?"

"Tea," I said, because I felt nauseous.

"Tea?" Ralph winked. "Did anyone ever tell you what a weird kid you are?"

The lady behind the counter gave me a searching look.

"I've been working on the first draft for the book," Ralph said, tucking his racing sheet into the back of his notebook. "Let me read this just to make sure that it sounds okay to you."

He began to read in a funny fake little-girl voice that nearly made me fall off my stool. " 'I don't know if I want to be a fiddler when I grow up. My name is Rosamond Cole. I am ten years old. I have been playing the violin for two years.' " He looked at me. "Is that okay?"

I nodded. So far every word of it was true.

"'I take two lessons a week. I study at the School of Music with Ms. Theodora Radzinoff. I love to play.'"

There it was. The first lie. This was my chance to say, "No, I do not love to play. I hate it. I'm bad at it. I only keep doing it because it's so important to Mom and Dad. I don't know what I'm playing most of the time." But I didn't say anything. Why? Because I'm a coward! A very little coward.

Also, because I love my poor mixed-up uncle Ralph, who goes and loses all his money at the racetrack and gets hollered at by my mom and always wants to have a good time and bring nice presents that cost much too much money. I knew that he was counting on me in a big way. I couldn't disappoint him.

After I finished my cup of tea, we both went to the School of Music. As usual, the dumbness coat came on me, but not as usual, T.R. greeted me with a hug. I could hardly believe it.

She had on lipstick. She had on perfume. She had on a new pair of earrings (hearts). She seemed to have an electrical current running through her. She laughed and leaped and smiled and clapped her hands and hummed. She was knocking her brains out to give me the best lesson in the world.

Uncle Ralph was hopping around as if the current turned him on too.

I was like the quiet ring of a three-ring circus.

When the lesson was over, T.R. said to U.R., "I am arranging the recital for May the twentieth. By then she should be ready. It shouldn't be a disaster at any rate, for me or for her."

"Who?" I said.

"You," said Radzinoff in a strained, smiling-through-her-teeth voice, "will play a solo at the spring recital."

"It will give the book its necessary

tension and climax," Uncle Ralph said. "I will follow you as you prepare for the big moment. Your recital."

Radzinoff said, "We will use the large room downstairs. It can hold about a hundred people. It has a lovely little stage. Rosamond will play in the chamber-music group, of course, and then she will perform her solo. She will have to work very hard, but I know she can do it. Just to be sure she does her best, I will give her a lesson *every weekday afternoon* until the concert."

Chapter Three

The next day an extremely peculiar thing started to happen to me. I began to feel great.

I know exactly where I was when this feeling began. I was sitting between Mom and Uncle Ralph in the shoe store. It was Friday afternoon, my half day at school. We had gone shopping for my recital dress and shoes. Mom had just bought me a beautiful pink dress with a black velvet bow in front. Mom and Uncle Ralph were arguing about which pair of shoes I should get.

"I want her to have the white ones," U.R. said.

"They are much too expensive," Mom said. U.R. closed his eyes. "I *never* consider price."

"And that is why you are always broke," Mom snapped. "There is no reason under the sun why you should be broke. You just throw all your money away at that silly racetrack and on a lot of overpriced junk. You need a partner to put some sense and order into your life, Ralph. How long do you think you can keep going like this? Rosamond is my last daughter."

"That's right." Uncle Ralph grabbed my hand. "My Rosy Dotes. My ace in the hole." He gave me a big, desperate wink. "Rosy's gonna make Ralphie flush again."

"For how long?" asked Mom. "You squandered all the Anitra and Pippa profits on nonsense. Horses."

"Wine, women, and song." Ralph was

red as a tomato. He called to the shoe salesman, "Wrap up the white patent. Nothing's too good for this little lady. She should have the best shoes in town. She is my rising star."

And all of a sudden that was just how I felt. Like a rising star.

Mom explained to the salesman that I was going to perform in a recital and my uncle was doing a book about me.

"I happen to be a pianist," the salesman said. Right away he could tell I wasn't just another snotty kid getting shoes. He really respected me.

My star got rings around it.

After we left the shoe store, U.R. and I went to my lesson. When we arrived, Radzy had on a new dress, new shoes, rouge, and nail polish. She had set up a tape recorder.

"I am going to tape your playing today, Rosy," she said. "Then when you come in on Monday, we can go over the tape and you can hear for yourself where you need to work and improve."

It made me feel like a famous artist to be taping my work. I loved it. Uncle Ralph took pictures of me playing for the tape recorder. He told Radzy she was a genius. Radzy told him he was the real genius. They seemed to forget I was there. Ralph told Radzy she was

a dynamite dame. He said that was the name of a horse he once bet on.

"I love horses," Radzy said. They made a date to go to the track. I said I guessed it was time to go home. I thought Uncle Ralph would take me for a soda. But he just waved.

Radzy blew me a kiss. "See you Monday, Rosamond. Have a good weekend."

Saturday morning I felt strange. I didn't have anything to do. Without Uncle Ralph and Radzy, I wasn't a star. I was bored.

"What's wrong, Rosy?" Mom said.

"I don't have anything to do," I said.

"What do you usually do on Saturday?"

"I'll go over to Hermione's," I said.

When Mrs. Wong opened the door to me, she rolled her eyes and said, "Hermione's in her room."

Hermione was standing in front of the full-length mirror on her closet door. She had an old white bed sheet draped around her and about a pound of make-up on her face. Beverly Sills was singing the Mad Scene from *Lucia di Lammermoor* on the record player.

Hermione was opening and closing her mouth and gesturing as if she were the one who was singing. She didn't notice me come in, so I sat down on her bed and waited for her to finish.

It was some performance. She waved her arms, she clutched the bed sheet, she tossed her head around, and she swayed and rocked. When Beverly Sills finished the last note, Hermione flung herself down on the floor with a big thud.

Mrs. Wong opened the door. "Hermione, are you all right?"

Hermione gathered the bed sheet around her and glared. "Lucia throws herself down a flight of stairs after that aria," she said. "I only threw myself on the floor."

"If you sing anything from *Peter Pan* I hope you'll know enough not to fly out the window," Mrs. Wong said, and she closed the door.

"She doesn't understand me," said Hermione.

"What is there to understand?" I said. "You just wave your arms around and open and close your mouth. I never saw anything so dumb in my life."

Hermione's face got narrow as if she had sucked all the air out of her cheeks. Her makeup showed up very bright. She looked like a kind of Muppet. In a Muppety voice she said, "Well, not all of us have been as lucky as *you*, Rosamond. If you would remember to tell your uncle Ralph about me, perhaps you would find out what a serious artist I really am."

"There's no luck to it," I said. "I happen to have star quality. Some people have star quality and some people don't. Waving your arms around in an old bed sheet and opening your mouth while somebody else sings the Mad Scene does not make you a star."

Then Hermione did something weird. She got up and punched me. I kicked her, and she fell down and couldn't get up because she was snagged in the bed sheet.

As I was going out her door, she yelled, "You're the worst violin player in school, Rosy Cole. Everybody knows it." She said a couple of other things too, but I was halfway down the hall.

Mrs. Wong poked her head out of the kitchen, and I ran for the front door.

As soon as I got home, I went to the bathroom to splash cold water on my face where Hermione had punched it. Mom followed me.

"What's up, Rosy?" She looked worried.

Then *I* did something I am not proud of. I still can't figure it out. I threw myself on my bed and began to hit my pillow.

"I won't be treated this way," I hollered. "I am a star. I am a book. Where is *my* photographer? Where is *my* coach? I need a session today."

Mom closed the door and tiptoed away. I heard her dial the telephone. "I know, Ralphie," she whispered. "But she's having a tantrum. Couldn't you take her just this once? You don't want her to blow the whole thing."

Mom came back to my room. "Good news, sweetheart. Uncle Ralph and Teddy have invited you to join them this evening for a concert at Carnegie Hall."

"That's more like it," I said.

Uncle Ralph and Teddy picked me up after dinner. I wore my new yellow-and-blue-print dress and my concert shoes. I had a yellow bow in my hair. Uncle Ralph photographed me stepping out the door and waving good-bye to Mom and Dad and Anitra and Pippa. Uncle Ralph said it would be a very good chapter to show me going out to a concert.

At Carnegie Hall I sat between Uncle Ralph and Teddy. At intermission Uncle Ralph photographed me in my seat and then in the lobby and then walking down the aisle. Someone asked me to autograph her program. I signed my name "Rosamond Cole, A Very Little Fiddler."

After the concert we went backstage to meet the musicians. Ralph took pictures of me. He took a picture of Teddy, too. "What's that for?" I said.

"Personal," Ralph said. For a minute

Teddy flashed me the old Radzy glare. When I was introduced to the violinist, I said I hoped one day to be standing in his place. He laughed out loud and Ralph took another picture.

In the taxi going home, I heard Radzy say to Ralph, "I think we have created a monster."

"A Very Little Monster," he said, and they both laughed. They were holding hands.

"Hey, cut that out," I said. "This is business." They looked at me as if they wished I would disappear, but of course they didn't say anything.

On Monday I was so excited about my lesson I didn't even stop for a soda. I ran up the steps of the School of Music two at a time. As I was climbing the inside stairs, I heard some poor clunk playing the violin. Playing *my* piece.

It was so awful it made me crack up. I thought, Boy, I was *never that bad*. Radzy must be having a fit. Who could it be?

Guess.

"I'm glad you're here early, Rose. I have been wanting to have a word with you privately. Sit down."

I sat down. My star *fell* down. In fact, it crashed and made one of those craters in the earth so that nothing was left but the black hole that swallowed it up.

"Let me level with you," Radzy said. "I have knocked my brains out to teach you. It's hopeless. You have no ear, no gift, no discipline. You have only one thing going for you." She took a deep breath and leaned toward me as if she were about to tell me a secret. "I'll clue you in. Your uncle Ralph is adorable, but he doesn't know anything but what he sees through his camera. So smile. Look as if you are having a wonderful time playing the violin."

"Okay," I agreed. Radzy and I were closing another secret deal. The only thing was, after hearing that tape, I couldn't do it. I couldn't pretend I was good. I couldn't look happy. I was miserable.

Chapter Four

That night, Anitra came into my room after dinner. She sat down on my bed and stretched her legs and started to do tiny pliés in the air.

"Rosy," she said softly, "something is the matter. You look awful. I told Mom and Dad, and they won't listen, but I know something is really bothering you."

"It is," I said.

"You don't have to tell me about it."
Anitra sat up all of a sudden. "I know.
Don't forget, I've been there. Me, and
Pippa too."

"I thought you loved it."

"At the time I did. Now I'm not so
sure. A lot of things happened that
made me miserable later. Other kids
talked behind my back and said I wasn't
really any good. I was hurt when the
book got bad reviews. I cried a lot. But
mostly I got very confused. I felt as if I
were being tested and I wasn't ready
yet."

"I know," I said. "Oh, Anitra, I know
exactly what you mean." I began to cry.
Anitra put her arms around me and we
sat like that on the bed.

"What can I do?" I said. "What can I
do?"

"I wish I knew," said Anitra. "Maybe
you should tell them what you think?"

I went to sleep that night feeling a little better. I didn't know what to do yet, but knowing that Anitra understood helped.

The next morning I talked to my reflection in the bathroom mirror. "Mom," I said to it, "I can't go through with Uncle Ralph's book or with the recital. I can't stand up on a stage and play for a hundred people. The idea makes me sick to my stomach." I grabbed my stomach and doubled over for dramatic impact. "Oh, please, please don't make me do it. I know how I sound. They'll throw things and laugh at me. Or maybe even cry like Mrs. Rapposo."

I brushed my teeth and walked down the hall to the kitchen. Mom and Dad were having breakfast.

"I can't go through with Uncle Ralph's book or with the recital," I said. I began to blubber.

"Now, Rosy." Mom got up and hugged me. "This is just a case of last-minute jitters."

"No, it isn't," I sobbed. "I can't play. I'm awful. I heard myself on the tape. How would you feel if it were you?"

"That's just it, honey." Mom beamed. "All my life I have wanted to be famous and well-known. That's why I've tried so hard to get those things for my girls."

I knew she could not understand. I went back to my room and looked at the calendar. I had ten days till the recital. I couldn't let another one go by. It was time to pack my book bag for school, but I didn't pack books. I took twenty dollars I had been saving up for a skateboard. Mom and Dad were getting dressed for work. I just called good-bye to them through the door.

Anitra and Pippa had left for school.

I kissed Pie and then I hit the road.

The road I hit headed west, which meant it took me through Central Park. It was a beautiful spring morning and I was running away from home.

I was running away from music.

But right away something told me you can't really run away from your problems. They follow you.

Then it came to me: THE BEST IDEA
OF MY LIFE. I didn't have to run away.

I ran home. I got dressed and went
back to the park.

A lot of people laughed. Some listened, some put their fingers in their ears. They signed my petition. I had the biggest crowd around.

People I knew saw me. The super of our building saw me. He gave me a quarter.

Pippa saw me. She came back with Anitra. Mrs. Rapposo saw me and burst out laughing. But in the middle of laughing, she froze like a statue. Anitra suddenly looked scared. Pippa put her hand over her mouth and said, "Uh-oh," and there was Mom.

Somebody must have called her at work, because she shouldn't have been in the park at that hour of the day. I had wanted to show her my petition when I had lots of names on it. I had *not* wanted her to see me getting the names. We looked at each other and I kept playing.

"Okay, Rose," Mom said softly. Then guess what? She stepped up to the table and signed my petition. "Let's go home now," she said. I folded up my stand and put my fiddle back in its case. My audience was leaving.

"You won," Pippa said.

"Triumphed," Anitra corrected.

We went home and took the carpet off the wall. Mom called T.R. and U.R. to tell them the news. I was taken out of the recital and withdrawn from lessons.

The next day T.R. sent me a note saying she was proud of my "guts."

Mrs. Rapposo sent me a box of candy and a note saying she was "grateful for my honesty."

In school, three people told me I wasn't their best friend anymore. Hermione still wouldn't speak to me. But what worried me most was Uncle Ralph.

I had let him down. I told Mom how worried I was.

"Oh, don't get upset about Ralph," Mom said. "He's all excited about a new book he's doing. It's a photographic story about a wonderful young racehorse. He's even picked out a title, but I can't remember it."

"*A Very Little Filly*," I said.

"How did you know?" Mom said.

"I think it's what he always wanted to do," I said.

"Teddy is helping him," said Mom, "so he won't lose whatever he makes before he makes it."

On the first Monday in June, I came home from school and found Uncle Ralph talking to Mom in the living room.

"Hi there, Rosy Dotes," he said. "How's about a big kiss and hug for

73

Uncle Ralph?" He gave me a big hug. "If not for you, I would never have met the luckiest bet of my life."

"Teddy Radzinoff," said Mom.

"Your new aunt," Uncle Ralph said.

I went right over to Hermione's to tell her the news. At first she said I couldn't come in, but soon we were sitting in the kitchen having cookies and milk and laughing over what had happened.

After that we went into Hermione's

room and put Beverly Sills on the record player. Hermione wrapped the bed sheet around her and opened and closed her mouth and waved her arms around while I pretended to be a famous photographer taking pictures. I hopped around going *click, click, click*.

After Hermione finished, we decided there would be a magnificent party for us. We dressed up in Mrs. Wong's fake pearls and diamonds from her junk-jewelry drawer. We put on her old fur wrap and her new velvet evening coat. We went into the kitchen and filled champagne glasses with seltzer, which we drank, and then pretended to be dizzy.

"Oh, dahlings," we called out to our millions of fans. "How too, too divine." We had such a terrific time, I wondered if Uncle Ralph could make a book out of us. I guessed he couldn't.

"We aren't Very Littles," I said.

"Or Teeny Weenies," Hermione said.

We were just Rose and Hermione, age ten.